Wilf came to play with Chip. They made
a rocket ship out of bits and pieces. The
rocket ship looked quite good.

1

Wilf and Chip played in the rocket ship.
They pretended to be spacemen.

"The rocket is going to take off," said
Wilf. "Five ... four ... three ... two ..."

Floppy ran up. He wanted to get in the rocket ship with Wilf and Chip.

"Go away, Floppy," called Chip. "The rocket is going to take off!"

Nadim came to play. He had his
computer with him, but he liked the look of
the rocket ship. He wanted to play in it too.

Just then, it began to rain.

"There's not room for all of us," said
Chip. "Let's go inside and play with
Nadim's computer."

They played a game on the computer. It was called Red Planet. They had to land a rocket on the planet. Wilf and Chip crashed the rocket. Nadim didn't. He was good at the game.

Suddenly, the magic key began to glow.
Chip and Wilf pulled Nadim away from
the computer and ran into Biff's room.

"Come on," called Chip. "It's time for
an adventure."

The magic took them to a rocket ship. It took Floppy too. The rocket looked as if it was about to take off, but the door was open. Nadim wanted to look inside the rocket.

"Come on," he called.
Chip didn't want to go inside. "It may not be safe," he said.

"Why not?" said Nadim. "This is a magic adventure."

They went inside the rocket. There was
nobody there.

"Look at this computer," said Nadim.
Floppy jumped up and put his paw on a
button.

Five … four … three … two … one. The
rocket began to take off. Up it went and
out into space.

"Oh no!" said Chip. "I don't know where
we're going."

They began to float about inside the rocket. Nadim found some boots. He put them on.

"We must put these boots on," he said. "They will keep us down on the floor."

They went to the window and looked
out. They saw a big red planet.

"We are going to land on that planet,"
said Nadim. "We will soon be there."

Nadim made the rocket land.

"I wouldn't like to do that again," he said.

"It's a good job Nadim knows about computers," thought Wilf. "I wouldn't like to crash here."

There was red dust all over the planet.
There were red rocks and red mountains.
Floppy didn't like the look of it. He began
to bark and bark.

"There are no trees," he thought.

They wanted to go outside and look at
the planet. They found a space buggy.
They looked in the space buggy and found
some spacesuits.

"Let's put these spacesuits on," said
Wilf. "Then we can go outside."

"Do you think it will be safe outside?"
asked Chip.

"I don't know," said Wilf.

They went out on the planet in the
buggy. The buggy bumped over the rocks
and the red dust flew up.

"I don't like this," thought Floppy. "I'm
not made for space adventures."

Suddenly the ground cracked and a big
hole opened up.

"Oh help," said Chip, Wilf, and Nadim
as the buggy fell into the hole.

They fell down and down inside the planet.

"I don't like this," thought Floppy. "I want to go home."

They all landed with a bump. The
buggy landed with a crash and broke in
two. They were inside a big cave.

"What a place!" said Wilf. "Look at it."
Chip looked at the buggy.

"It's broken," he said. "It's had it!"

"How will we get back to the rocket?"

Floppy began to bark. There were some
creatures in the cave. They looked like
funny little people.

"Oh no!" said Nadim. "Look at them! I
hope they like us."

The creatures looked at the boys. They
climbed on the broken buggy and pulled
out a spacesuit. One of them turned a tap
on Floppy's spacesuit.

Floppy's spacesuit began to fill with air. It got bigger and bigger. Then Floppy began to float.

"Get Floppy!" yelled Chip. "Don't let him float away!"

Wilf asked the creatures how to get out of the cave. They told him that there was no way out. They said that they had never been outside.

Wilf had a good idea. He took a
spacesuit out and he filled it with air. The
spacesuit got bigger and bigger. It began
to float up and up.

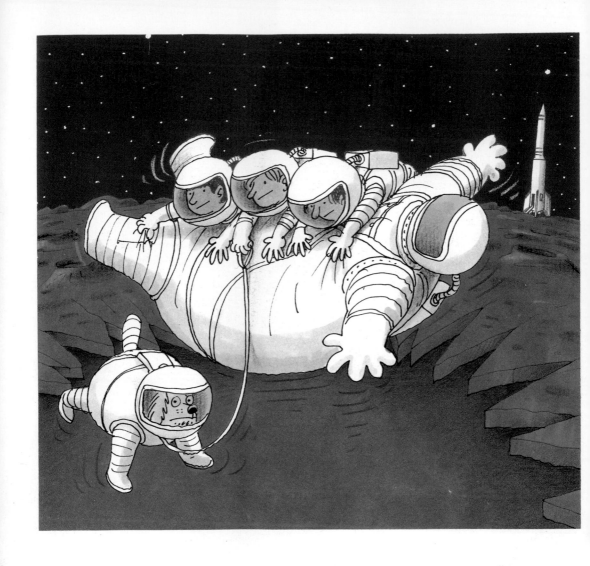

"Hold on," called Wilf, "and don't let go!"

The spacesuit floated up out of the cave.

"We can float back to the rocket," said Chip. "What a good idea!"

"I hope it won't go pop," thought Floppy.

They floated back to the rocket. Wilf let the air out of the spacesuit and it came down to the ground.

"Good old Wilf!" said Nadim.

"I don't like floating," thought Floppy.

They went inside the rocket and it took off. Nadim turned on the computer and looked at the screen.

"We'll soon be home," he said.

Just then the magic key began to glow.
"That's good," thought Floppy. "They
won't have to land the rocket. Dogs don't
like space adventures."

The magic took them back home.

"I liked that adventure," said Wilf.
He looked at the little spacesuit.

"So did I," said Nadim, "but I'm glad I
didn't have to land that rocket again."